PIC MacCar
McCartney, Tania,
An English year : twelve months in
the life of England's kids /
17.99

3 4028 09583 8661
HARRIS COUNTY PUBLIC LIBRARY

D1368683

WITHDRAWN

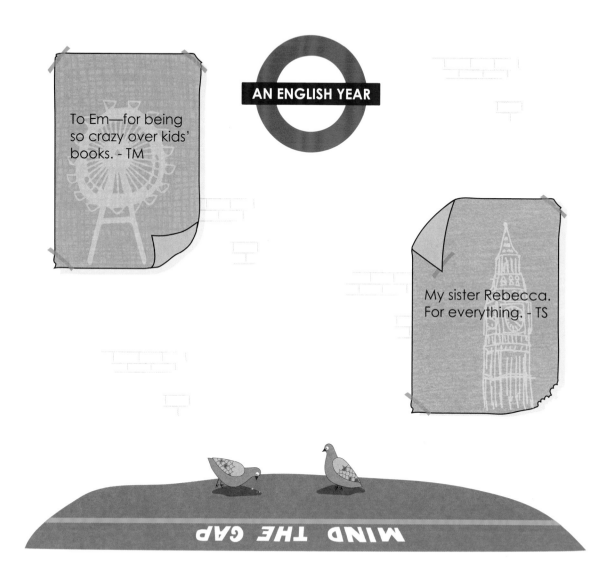

AN ENGLISH YEAR

TWELVE MONTHS IN THE LIFE OF ENGLAND'S KIDS

TANIA MCCARTNEY + TINA SNERLING

Welcome to England

Hello, I'm VICTORIA. My family has owned land in England for many generations. I love riding my pony, having picnics in our garden and visiting my great aunt at the seaside. I'm nine and when I'm an adult, I want to raise horses on my farm.

Namaste! I'm AMAN. I'm ten and my family arrived from India just before I was born. My favourite sports are cricket and rowing. I also love maths, computers and listening to music on my phone. One day, I want to be a games creator.

Hi, I'm TANDI and my grandparents were born in Jamaica. I was born in England. I love painting, athletics and making cool science experiments. I'm seven, and when I grow up, I want to be a scientist.

Hiya, I'm GEORGE and I'm six. I have three big brothers and we like to kick the ball in the street and in the park. I love football, cooking with Mum and playing on my iPad. When I grow up, I want to be a pro footballer.

Witam! I'm AMELIA and I'm eight years old. My mum, dad and I came to England three years ago, and I'm still learning English. I love my new school, my friends, reading and making things. One day, I would like to be a teacher.

January

January is COLD and wet and dark.

It's NEW YEAR'S DAY! We have a big roast dinner.

ROAST VEGGIES

BEEF

GRAVY

YORKSHIRE PUDDINGS

We love to play boardgames.

PUZZLES

GAMES

We eat hot CHESTNUTS from a paper bag.

It's back to SCHOOL.

xmas decorations

It's TWELFTH NIGHT. We take down our Christmas tree to avoid bad luck.

09 SCHOOL BUS

We walk, catch the BUS or get a lift to school.

On SNOW days, we don't go to school.

We have CORGIS, just like the Queen!

WOOF! WOOF!

During PONGAL, Indian people give thanks for the harvest.

HAPPY PONGAL

We have DINNER around the family table.

MUSHY PEAS + CHIPS

FISH FINGERS

PORK CUTLETS

PASTA

CURRY

JERK CHICKEN

COTTAGE PIE

SAUERKRAUT + POTATO

At Chinese New Year, there are FIREWORKS and parades in Manchester and other cities. Sometimes, celebrations fall in February.

February

Six Nations RUGBY begins.

Dad makes BACON butties.

Mmmmmm ...

The first SNOWDROPS appear in our garden.

On PANCAKE DAY, people flip pancakes while running down the street!

PASS-THE-PARCEL

MUSICAL CHAIRS

PIÑATA

At BIRTHDAY PARTIES, we play lots of games.
Dad tries to give us The Bumps!

We get BUSY after school.

BALLET

CUB SCOUTS AND BROWNIES

JUDO

GYMNASTICS

We have a short school HOLIDAY.

Mum BAKES Victoria sponge and apple crumble.

On VALENTINE'S DAY, we give cards to our sweethearts.

DOLL HOUSE

LEGO

IPAD

When it's COLD outside, we play by the radiator.

March

Grandad takes us FISHING in the river.

We pick BLUEBELLS and press them into books.

We fossick for four-leaf clovers on ST PATRICK'S DAY.

TEA
FLOWERS
GIFTS
CARDS

On MOTHER'S DAY, we spoil Mum with gifts and cards. We take her out for high tea.

It's COMMONWEALTH Day.

UNDERGROUND

MIND THE GAP

We catch the TUBE into town.

We ride bikes or KICK A BALL outside after school.

WOOF!

People prep their pooches for CRUFTS, the world's largest dog show.

Our RABBITS live in a hutch in the garden. We also have a cat and a budgie.

HOLI is the Spring Festival of Colours. We cover each other in coloured paint.

CLOCKS GO FORWARD

British SUMMER Time begins.

Some years, EASTER falls in March.

April

①

It's APRIL FOOLS' DAY. Dad talks of cows that make strawberry milk!

HOT CROSS BUNS!
HOT CROSS BUNS!
ONE A PENNY, TWO A PENNY
HOT CROSS BUNS!

On GOOD FRIDAY, we eat hot cross buns with melty butter.

We have school HOLIDAYS for Easter.

There's lots to eat at EASTER.

EASTER BUNS WITH CHEESE

ROAST LAMB + MINT SAUCE

BABKA

SIMNEL CAKE

Pisanki eggs are DECORATED with traditional designs.

Time for an EGG HUNT!

Mum grows HERBS on the kitchen window sill.

On EASTER MONDAY, we go egg rolling and watch Morris Dancers.

BASIL

ROSEMARY   DILL

PARSLEY

It's ST GEORGE'S DAY.

23

It's the GRAND NATIONAL horse race.

TO BE OR
NOT TO BE?

William SHAKESPEARE was born.

On WEEKENDS, we go pond dipping.

Dad runs the London MARATHON
in a whacky costume.

May

It's MAY DAY.

We have a short school HOLIDAY.

We CLIMB TREES and do cartwheels on the grass.

OLE OLE OLE!

Blossoms abound at the stunning Chelsea FLOWER Show.

1ST

YOGHURT

CRISPS

SANDWICHES

WRAP

FRUIT

We take our LUNCH to school or have a school dinner at the canteen.

We shout and cheer for the FA CUP FINAL.

It's lovely having TEA PARTIES in the garden.

On the weekends, we go swimming or play TENNIS or netball.

Horses gallop at the POLO.

COOPER'S HILL

It's SPRING BANK holiday.
We chase cheese at Cooper's Hill!

TUDOR STYLE

PITCHED ROOF

THATCHING

We ride our BIKES in the sunshine.

Our HOUSE is 500 years old!

June

We love to SWIM in summer!

The family goes CAMPING. We always get wet.

IT'S RAINING AGAIN...

THAT'S THE WAY TO DO IT!

Punch and Judy
Puppet show
starts midday

Punch and Judy PUPPET SHOWS always make us laugh.

We eat FISH AND CHIPS at the seaside.

We have strawberries and cream at the WIMBLEDON tennis championships.

It's the Queen's birthday celebration. We watch TROOPING THE COLOUR on telly.

Henley Royal REGATTA.

It's suits and ginormous hats for ROYAL ASCOT.

It's FATHER'S DAY and we love to spoil our dad.

PINT OF LAGER

ROAST DINNER

SOCKS

UNDIES

We GOBBLE Jaffa Cakes and Jammie Dodgers.

We make DAISY CHAINS and wear them in our hair.

On MIDSUMMER'S DAY, people go to Stonehenge to see the sun rise.

July

OUT!

Test CRICKET begins.

£1.00

strawberry jam

Mum makes SCONES and jam for the local fair.

Granny grows RED ROSES in her garden.

It's very noisy at the British GRAND PRIX!

We help Dad build a TREEHOUSE in the old oak tree.

During the mid-summer festival of WIANKI, wreaths float down the river.

We go for PICNICS in the countryside.

Eid al-Fitr marks the end of RAMADAN. No more fasting! Ramadan can fall in other months, too.

BOBBIES help us cross busy London streets.

AFTERNOON!

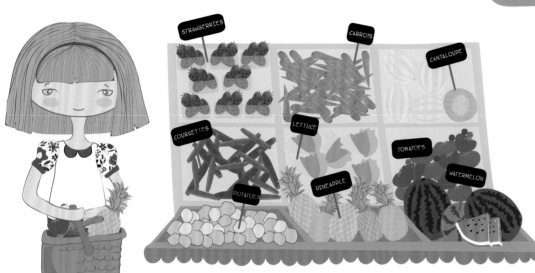

STRAWBERRIES

CARROTS

CANTALOUPE

COURGETTES

LETTUCE

TOMATOES

POTATOES

PINEAPPLE

WATERMELON

We buy fruit and vegetables from the TOWN MARKET on Saturdays.

The Manchester Children's BOOK FESTIVAL is the coolest.

PEACH

BLACKCURRANT

LEMONADE

COLA

FIZZY DRINKS and squash are refreshing!

We start SUMMER HOLIDAYS!

August

During the summer holidays, we go to Spain or just head to the SEASIDE.

It's International YOUTH Day. **12**

At bedtime, it's still LIGHT outside!

open

BUCKINGHAM PALACE is open to the public. We see the Changing of the Guard.

The FOOTBALL season begins!

We pick BLACKBERRIES and try not to eat them on the way home.

We practise RUGBY in the park.

We help Mum HARVEST the vegetable garden.

FRENCH HORN

TRUMPET

CELLO

We slurp ICE LOLLIES to cool down.

Granny and Grandad go to THE PROMS.

It's August BANK HOLIDAY.

September

The SCHOOL year begins.

We wear UNIFORMS.

It's AUTUMN. Leaves start turning GOLD.

HEE HAW!

In the morning, we love cereal and toast.
Dad likes a cooked breakfast.

CRUMPETS WITH JAM

SUNNY SIDE UP

DAD

PORRIDGE

SAUSAGES, EGGS
AND BAKED BEANS

PARATHA WITH VEGETABLES
AND YOGHURT

During Blackpool Illuminations,
we ride DONKEYS on the beach.

DUCKS quack on the river.

QUACK!

We go to the pub garden with Dad and have packets of CRISPS.

The British SCIENCE Festival is held in Birmingham.

BUBBLE AND SQUEAK

We have really cool MEALS with really strange names.

SARNIES

TOAD-IN-THE-HOLE

BANGERS AND MASH

It's HARVEST FESTIVAL. There's singing and baskets of food and braided bread. We donate food to charity.

FOOTBALL

At school, we play lots of SPORTS.

TENNIS

CRICKET

October

The WEATHER cools down.

There's a short school holiday BREAK.

It's WORLD TEACHERS' DAY.

British Summer TIME ends.

CLOCKS GO BACK

WATCH OUT FOR STINGING NETTLES!

Time for LEAF DIVING in the park.

We love spotting SQUIRRELS and red robins.

We climb over stiles to visit our FRIENDS.

After school, we do homework or go to the park or bounce on the TRAMPOLINE.

On weekends, we make MUD PIES.

CANDLES

FIREWORKS

LANTERNS

DIWALI explodes with light.

BOBBING FOR APPLES

PUMPKIN CARVING

TRICK OR TREATING

DRESSING UP

31

At HALLOWEEN, we dress up in costumes and gather sweets.

We play CONKERS.

NOVEMBER

It's almost **DARK** when we get home from school.

The mornings are FROSTY. Winter is coming.

REMEMBER REMEMBER THE FIFTH OF NOVEMBER!

JACKET POTATOES

TOASTED MARSHMALLOWS

On **BONFIRE NIGHT**, we wrap up warmly.

WHAT'S FOR PUDDING?

TREACLE PUDDING

BREAD + BUTTER PUDDING

CUSTARD

Granny makes delicious **DESSERTS**.

MAKE A WISH!

Mum makes the Christmas pudding on STIR-UP SUNDAY.

We make PIES from orchard fruit.

Sometimes our washing FREEZES on the line.

On REMEMBRANCE DAY, we remember those who died at war. We wear red poppies.

SWEETS are delicious.

We raise MONEY at school for BBC Children In Need.

20

It's UNIVERSAL CHILDREN'S DAY.

As the weather cools down, we love to stay inside and get CRAFTY.

December

WINTER arrives.

Mum makes FRUIT MINCE pies and mulled wine.

RED

LIGHTS

FIR TREE
CANDY CANES
BAUBLES

WREATH

STOCKINGS

Christmas holidays begin. We visit the Christmas LIGHTS in town.

We sing Christmas CAROLS and decorate the house with festive fun.

ADVENT begins. We open little boxes and find treats inside.

1 2 3 4 5 6
7 8 9 10 11
12 13 14 15 16
17 18 19 20
21 22 25 23 24

XMAS

Father Christmas scoots down the CHIMNEY so we need to make sure the fire is out!
We leave him milk and biscuits, and carrots for his reindeer.

It's CHRISTMAS DAY. We eat a roast dinner and listen to the Queen's Christmas message.

ROAST TURKEY

YULE LOG

GRAVY   VEGETABLES   CHRISTMAS PUDDING

Jewish people light the MENORAH in Trafalgar Square.

We dress up for JUNKANOO.

On BOXING DAY, we eat leftovers and watch *The Snowman* on telly.

HE'S BEHIND YOU!

The local PANTOMIME is awesome.

On NEW YEAR'S EVE, we count down with Big Ben.

We sing AULD LANG SYNE to farewell another grand year.

Our Country

I SPY A GREAT COUNTRY!

OUR GEOGRAPHIC COUNTIES

Bedfordshire
Berkshire
Bristol
Buckinghamshire
Cambridgeshire
Cheshire
City of London
Cornwall + Isles of Scilly
Cumbria
Derbyshire
Devon
Dorset
Durham
East Riding of Yorkshire
East Sussex
Essex

Gloucestershire
Greater London
Greater Manchester
Hampshire
Herefordshire
Hertfordshire
Isle of Wight
Kent
Lancashire
Leicestershire
Lincolnshire
Merseyside
Norfolk
North Yorkshire
Northamptonshire
Northumberland

Nottinghamshire
Oxfordshire
Rutland
Shropshire
Somerset
South Yorkshire
Staffordshire
Suffolk
Surrey
Tyne and Wear
Warwickshire
West Midlands
West Sussex
West Yorkshire
Wiltshire
Worcestershire

We drink more TEA per person than anyone else in the WORLD!

England has an awesome history!

A huge thank you to English Advisor Emma Perry and to the kids of Corsham Regis Primary Academy. Also to the team at Exisle and most particularly publisher Anouska Jones for her continued insight and eagle editing eye. TM + TS

First published 2015

EK Books
an imprint of Exisle Publishing Pty Ltd
Inverwick House, Albert Street, Nairn,
IV12 4HE, Scotland, UK
'Moonrising', Narone Creek Road,
Wollombi, NSW 2325, Australia
P.O. Box 60-490, Titirangi
Auckland 0642, New Zealand
www.ekbooks.com.au

Copyright © 2015 in text: Tania MCartney
Copyright © 2015 in illustrations: Tina Snerling
Tania McCartney and Tina Snerling assert the moral right to be identified as the authors of this work.

All rights reserved. Except for short extracts for the purpose of review, no part of this book may be reproduced, stored in a retrieval system or transmitted in any form or by any means, whether electronic, mechanical, photocopying, recording or otherwise, without prior written permission from the publisher.

A CiP record for this book is available from the National Library of Australia

ISBN 978 1 921966 86 6

Designed and typeset by Tina Snerling
Typeset in Century Gothic, Street Cred and custom fonts
Printed in China
This book uses paper sourced under ISO 1 4001 guidelines from well-managed forests and other controlled sources.

10 9 8 7 6 5 4 3 2 1

Author Note

This is by no means a comprehensive listing of the events and traditions celebrated by England's multitude of ethnic people. The entries in this book have been chosen to reflect a range of modern lifestyles for the majority of English children, with a focus on traditional 'English' elements and themes, which are in themselves a glorious mishmash of present, past, introduced and endemic culture. Content in this book has been produced in consultation with a native English Advisor, school teacher, and school children, with every intention of respecting the cultural and idiosyncratic elements of England and its people.

Harris County Public Library, Houston, TX